BEAR GOES TO TOWN

Anthony Browne

D1080824

SPARROW
BOOKS

Other books in the Sparrow Picture Book series

Crazy Charlie   Ruth Brown
If Mice Could Fly   John Cameron
The Tiger Who Lost his Stripes   Michael Foreman
Not Now, Bernard   David McKee
Tusk Tusk   David McKee
The Adventures of King Rollo   David McKee
Further Adventures of King Rollo   David McKee
The Hunter and the Animals   Tomie de Paola
Puss in Boots   Tony Ross
Goldilocks and the Three Bears   Tony Ross
Emergency Mouse   Bernard Stone & Ralph Steadman
Inspector Mouse   Bernard Stone & Ralph Steadman

A Sparrow Book

Published by Arrow Books Limited

17-21 Conway Street, London W1P 6JD

An imprint of the Hutchinson Publishing Group
London Melbourne Sydney Auckland Johannesburg and agencies
throughout the world

First published by Hamish Hamilton 1982
Sparrow edition 1983

© Anthony Browne 1982

Printed and bound in Great Britain by
Blantyre Printing & Binding Ltd
London and Glasgow

ISBN 0 09 932040 1

One day Bear went to town.

There were a lot of people rushing about. It was rush hour. Bear was small and people could not see him. They knocked him down.

Bear saw big yellow eyes looking down at him.

"What is that?" asked Cat looking at Bear's pencil.

"It's my magic pencil," said Bear.

"Then draw me something to eat," said Cat.

Bear drew lots of different kinds of food.
"Will that do?" Bear asked.
"Yes, thank you," said Cat and gobbled everything up.
Bear and Cat stood outside a butcher's shop.

Bear did not like the look of the butcher.

Bear and Cat stood outside a bear shop.
"I wonder if people eat them," thought Bear.
Look out, Cat!

HELP . . . !

Cat was thrown into a van. Bear drew himself a pair of roller skates and hurried after him.

The van turned into a gateway and stopped in a yard.

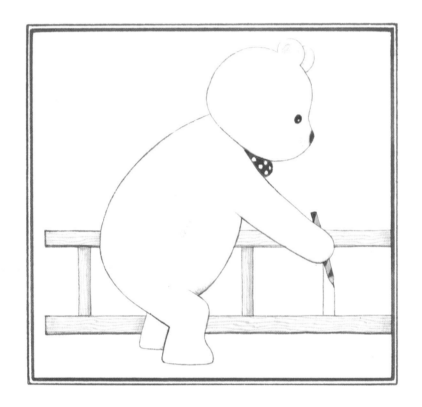

The driver locked Cat in a shed.
"Mmmm. Most odd," muttered Bear. As the
guard's back was turned, Bear went round to the
side of the building and drew himself a ladder.

Bear got to work with his pencil again and sawed through the bars on the shed window.

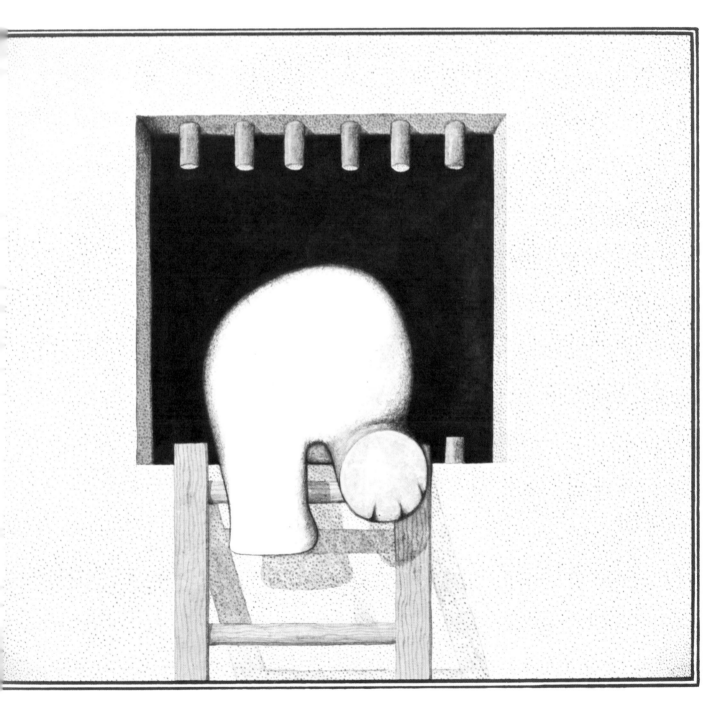

He climbed in.

"You took your time," Cat said.

"What is this place?" Bear asked.
"We don't know," said Cow, "but can you get
us out?"

Bear used his pencil. "Follow me," he said.

Sheep refused to leave.

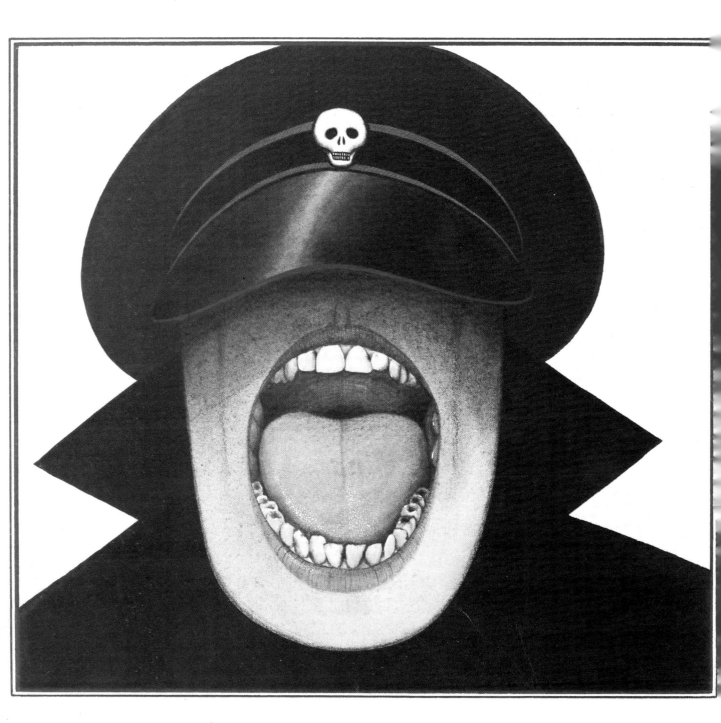

STOP!!!

Guards chased the animals across the yard.

"Banana skins, I think," said Bear and began to draw.

Whooooooops.

Look out behind you, Bear!

"Tacks, I think," said Bear and drew some.

Psssssssss.

The animals got away.

"Where are we?" asked Cockerel.
"In the middle of nowhere," Bear replied.
"I like it here," said Pig.
"We don't want to be eaten . . .
". . . or beaten," added Dog.
"Yes, it's a dog's life," sighed Cat.
"Easy," said Bear and began to draw.

"Thank you, Bear."

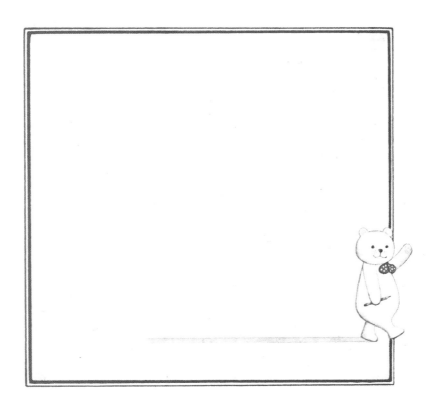

And Bear walked on.